CONTENTS

	Prologue	1
1	June 1st	Pg. 2
2	June 2nd	Pg. 5
3	June 5th	Pg. 12
4	June 6th	Pg. 18
5	June 7th	Pg. 27
6	June 8th	Pg. 33
7	June 9th	Pg. 35
8	June 10th	Pg. 37
9	June 11th	Pg. 38
10	June 12th	Pg. 39
11	June 15th	Pg. 41
12	June 16th	Pg. 42
13	June 20th	Pg. 59
14	July 3rd	Pg. 62

The Diary of a Lost Girl Lost

Nina M. Noss

Copyright © 2017 Nina M. Noss

All rights reserved.

ISBN:
9781521945391

PROLOGUE

How do you begin to piece together the shattered shards of a broken life? When the foundations of everything around you come crumbling down and you are left utterly exposed to the harsh realities of life, where then do you start? To be thrust so suddenly onto a new path, out of the shadows and into the light, how do you keep your footing and not fall? To not be dragged down by the chains and shackles that you will not, or cannot yet release? Does the past define who you are, what you are to become? Are you labelled only by what you have survived, a victim or a survivor? Can you not just be alive?

When you feel like you are standing on the edge of a cliff; before you, a vast open ocean; behind you, a fierce tidal wave. The first represents the future, a glimmer of hope for a new start, many miles away on the horizon; all you have to do is jump and let the current take you on its course. The later, represents the haunting, harrowing memories of a past you are so desperate to be free of, yet remains shackled to you, locked with no key. No matter how far you run, it is always there. There is one choice before you; step forward, or step back. Step forward and you have a chance, all you have to do is take the leap and trust you will avoid all rocks on the way down, then believe you can navigate the merciless waves as they crash upon the cliff side. Take a step backwards, and you'll be swept away by the past, engulfed by its power and resilience, a hopeless, impossible battle of keeping head above water. Or do you take the third option? Take neither a step backwards or a step forwards. A lifetime stuck in one spot, surviving, not living. Frozen in time blinded to what lies ahead and yet denying what is coming up behind?

Only time will tell......

JUNE 1ST 2017

The light of the moon illuminated my room with an eerie presence, the window, wedged open with a stick allowed a light evening breeze to sway the curtains, towards me, then away, the repeating movement held my gaze, it relaxed me into a false sense of contentment, the same way waves rushing upon the shore could do to others. But only momentarily because it was a very dangerous thing to feel here, always on my toes I had to be to survive. I took what little pleasure from the moment I could for with night time came terrors beyond imaging, there in that forsaken place, well, at least for me. It was warm, very warm, and as I sat atop my covers I was grateful for the gentle gust as it brushed my face. Then I heard it, that dreadful sound of heavy boots hitting the floor of the corridor outside my room. They grew louder. A fierce chill went down my spine. Was it time already? I began to sweat; I jumped under the covers despite the heat, trying to get any comfort for my growing terror. However, it was folly; I knew very well the thin sheets would do nothing. It wouldn't stop him. I was alone and a prisoner to his will. The boots stopped, my breathing intensified, my whole body started to shake. I heard the chain rattle as he removed the keys from his belt, slowly. He knew I'd be trembling, that's how he liked it though, he got a thrill from inflicting fear into the innocent and inflicting fear into me was his mastery. The key turned slowly; the handle rattled and the door creaked open. My silent trembling became whimpers as I heard him snigger above me.

"You never fail to disappoint me." He laughed, his voice deep, his rich Russian accent rolling out over the silence of the night. I'd stopped breathing in an attempt to hold in my whimpers, which were closely becoming full blown sobs by then. "After all these years, you still resist me. Why?" He taunted me, unbuckling his belt. I had to let out a breath as I heard the leather sliding against the denim of his jeans, the buckle jangled as he left it hanging by his side. I'd returned to silence, frozen with fear. The same process nearly every night, it had become a sort of ritual, the same movements, the same words, the same sniggering, and taunting, chilling process, it never gets any easier though.

'It will soon be over' I told myself every night, a weak substitute for a prayer, just something to help myself. True prayer, I'd learned never worked. I'd lost my faith in God long ago. He never came when I called. He never saved me. I was alone. I knew it, and he knew it.

"No-one's coming for you girl. No-one. So, stop your whining and come out from under the covers." he said as he rubbed his hand over the covers, down my side from my shoulder to my hip, he let his hand rest there. My body exploded in goose-bumps and they weren't the good kind. He squeezed my hip slightly as he unbuttoned his jeans with his other hand; I heard the zip being pulled down. I started shaking again. I knew I wouldn't for much longer, fear and hatred would stop that.

"Come on, don't keep me waiting." he turned me over so I was lying on my back, my eyes unwillingly met his, dark and unwelcoming, they sparkled with malice and lust. As he licked his lips, the candle flickered on my bedside table and illuminated the scar on his face, it made him seem evil and taller in the darkness. He pulled the covers away from me and returned his hand to my thigh; he made his way upwards under my nightdress. I flinched at his touch and felt sick to my stomach, as I turned my face away from his I felt his other hand make a strong, stinging contact with my face, burning, it brought tears to my eyes; he slapped me, a punishment for looking away. He grabbed my chin and turned me towards him as he climbed on top of me.

"Look at me girl; I want to see the fear in your eyes." He lowered and the pressure of his body on top of mine suffocated me. I felt his warm breath on my ear as he whispered, "are you ready?" and not waiting for an answer he proceeded with his task. I starred up at the celling as he lowered his face to my shoulder, all I could do was hope that someone would soon save me from this hell. Anyone. But I knew no-one would come, they hadn't yet, and I was entirely alone.

JUNE 2ND 2017

I heard a bell toll in the distance, morning had arrived already and with it another day. The gentle rays of the rising summer sun warmed my face as it shone through the open curtains. I always slept with the curtains open. I hated the dark. It reminded me too painfully of the small, cold, and windowless room I spent many months in when he first bought me here all, those years ago; down in the cellar where there was no light, no breeze on my skin. How old I was when he took me from my real home I couldn't remember. I have forgotten the face of my parents, and any memories from my life before here are very sparse. Another time, a different girl. I often think of what my childhood would have been like, carefree and normal, but they are just dreams. Growing up dreams like that helped me through, they gave me hope, now however, they are just agonising images of what could have been, of what I can never have, so now I try to push them from my mind as soon as they come knocking at the door.

As the rays hit my face, I began to hum a tune, one that always came to me after those terrible nights, how I knew it or where I first heard it I couldn't recall, but I liked to think it was from a time when my mum or dad sung me to sleep, safely tucked up in bed with no worries or no fears. I found it a comfort, if only a small comfort but it was a comfort none the less and I used it as often as I could.

I desperately desired a shower, I wanted to clean the filth of him off me, I hated it, and it made me feel so dirty. My door he always kept locked; he monitored everything I did by cameras he'd placed inside my room. I tried to wash myself the best I could from the bowl of water and a cloth that was left on the small table in the corner of my room. It did little to refresh me after the horrors of the previous night, so I sat back on my bed and looked out the window, hoping for anything to pass by that would distract me from the dark and gloomy recesses of my mind. A blue bird had made his home in the tree outside my window, I sat and watched it as it flew from branch to branch, chirping happily as it went about his morning business, in some ways, it was the only friend I had. It flew away suddenly as a loud bang startled both of us from the door behind me, it was unexpected and I jumped off my bed so quickly I landed awkwardly and fell against the window sill, cutting my chin, a few drops of blood dripped onto the floor. I stumbled up and barely got to my feet before he'd burst right through the door. He walked over to me and grabbed my arm roughly.

"What have you been doing to yourself?" he was very bad tempered this morning, I didn't answer him. He took my silence as an invitation to carry on, doomed if I talked, doomed if I didn't. "Didn't beat you around enough last night I see?" he paused; the side of his mouth curved upwards, "I'll be sure to fix that next time." He pushed me roughly out the room and then down the corridor. The house was un-kempt in many places, almost shack-like in many respects, wooden, cold, and not homely; but then, this isn't my home, just a prison and for that it lived up well to its name.

We were on the third floor of the house, it had four in total, plus the cellar, but I never went down there, not only did I have no desire to go down there, but if I attempted to I'm sure my captor would have beaten me even worse than he normally did. As he took me along the third floor we passed two other doors, what was behind them I never knew. One I was sure had to lead up to the floor above. I never went up there either. The second must have been a room of some kind, an occupied room it seemed because as we passed I glimpsed a shadow behind the door; it was pacing back and forth; they were gentle steps, unlike the harsh, pounding steps of my captor. The shadow paused and then moved away. I'd paused without realising when I saw the shadow; my captor stopped behind me, looked towards the door, and pushed me onwards. Not a word was said but his grip on my arm intensified.

He only let go of my arm when we reached the kitchen. He walked over to the window, looked out and pulled the blind down. Next, he made for the back door, opened it briefly then peered out and observed all directions clearly satisfied with what he saw, or didn't see. He was behaving very strangely, almost as though he was afraid of something. He closed the back door which lead to the large grounds and the gravel pathway to the drive, and locked it. The door had a glass pane in it, and a blind covering that, which he pulled down too. He turned abruptly and looked at me. Madness alight in his eyes, he scratched the stubble on his face and glimpsed towards the corner of the room. Until that moment, it had escaped my notice but lying on the floor, under a black plastic sheet I saw something that froze the blood in my veins. Hanging out from under the sheet was a hand, bloodied, black, and most definitely not moving. I gasped and as if expecting it, he was across the table, standing behind me and had his hand over my mouth all in the time it took me to decide to scream.

"Don't. Make. A. Sound." He spat, "one squawk from you and you'll end up just like her." Still holding me he moved over to the door that leads down to the cellar. That movement ignited bad memories, the day he bought me up those stairs he was holding me very much in the same way, hand over my mouth so I wouldn't scream for help, arms pinned by my sides. So much time had passed, but nothing had changed, not really. He fumbled with a key in his pocket and struggled to get it into the lock. He opened the door and pushed me down the stairs. I fell, thump, thump, thump, all the way to the bottom. The stairs were steep, and I felt awfully bruised as I lay on the floor. The fall had winded me terribly and I struggled to get my breath about as much as he struggled to control his temper. He grabbed me by the hair and dragged me to my feet. The tears started to roll down my cheeks.

The cellar was very dull, the walls were a grey cement colour; the floor, also cement, was covered in small puddles scattered around from the leaking pipes. The cellar hadn't changed much at all, and I now stood outside the same cell I was held in. There were six doors down there, each owner to a small, cube room; one steal door, no windows; two small hatches to each door; multiple locks. Hell. He opened the door we were standing in front of and pushed me inside, I fell to my knees and there was a small splash and to my horror, I saw that I had fallen into blood. I was kneeling in blood and a lot of it. I looked up, there was blood splattered across the wall and just in front of me was a large cutting knife, covered in blood. I grabbed my stomach and vomited where I knelt. I looked to my left, there lay four fingers. I vomited again and started shaking uncontrollably. While this happened, my captor simply stood behind me silent, his expression, un-readable.

"Clean it up." He dropped a mop down beside me. "I don't want one single drop of blood left anywhere in this room. You have two hours." He turned to leave but stopped and turned back to me, "and if you don't want to end up like her, with your blood splattered across these walls then make sure you don't leave this room." He turned around and walked back up to the kitchen, I heard the cellar door slam and lock. I was trapped down there again, alone. I sat back on my feet for a moment, trying to keep from vomiting a third time. I'd eaten so little I really didn't think I'd have any more to bring up. I tried to take deep breaths but the rancid smell of iron and sick did nothing to alleviate the sickness stirring in my stomach. I started scrubbing the floor. The bucket of water he left soon turned a deep red. The time passed and I barely registered anything I was doing. Shock had kicked in and my body was moving on its own. Eventually the room was clean, the smell of cleaning disinfectant blended with the scents of iron and vomit still in the air made me feel so faint I ran out of the room and leant against the door opposite. I leant on my knees to steady myself, and when I opened my eyes I saw a small piece of white paper being pushed out from underneath the door. There was someone else down there, trapped like I was! I picked up the note and tried to say something but the shock took my voice once again. I looked down the room to the other doors and I started to wonder about the other rooms, were there others trapped down there too, other girls? I heard the door unlock behind me and I quickly tried to put the note into my pocket. The door opened and a man walked down the stairs, but it wasn't my captor. His shadow as he stood in the dark bought back a memory; he was the man I'd often seen around the grounds from my window. I stood transfixed, and very afraid. He walked up to me, his face was very like my captor, but it wasn't as hard or unkind, he had a softer expression, a friendlier sparkle, seriously lacking the malice I was so used to.

We stood in silence, staring at each other until he said "Hurry up and put that in your pocket. Don't let him know that you have it. Keep it out of sight. Quickly", I didn't realise I was holding the note out to him, I looked down at it and still in shock from the events of the day I looked up at him and said,

"I don't have any pockets." If it were possible for my face to go any redder than it was from the poor woman's blood which I was covered in, I think I would have exploded from embarrassment. Then something new happened to me in that moment, I felt a fluttering that I'd never felt before, a giddiness came over me which increased when he smiled gently and moved closer.

"Give it to me." He whispered and held out his hand, I hesitated. How could I trust him? What if he gave it straight to my captor? I'd be as dead as that poor girl lying on the kitchen floor above. But what choice did I have? I considered his eyes and realised I had to trust him, if I didn't, I was dead anyway. I slowly gave him the note. He took it, put it in his pocket and gently took my arm. "Quietly now, I'm to take you back upstairs." with that he led the way back up into the kitchen, past the body and onwards to the third floor. He didn't take me straight back to my room. Instead he stopped outside the shower room, and took me inside. He turned on the shower, and removed a couple of cockroaches that were roaming around in the tub.

"Take a shower, clean the blood off your face. Don't leave the room; I'll get you some clean clothes." I was so desperate to clean the filth of the day and of the night before off that running didn't cross my mind, I got into the shower and I hadn't felt that good in a long time. I didn't hear him come back into the room but when I turned the shower off and was just about to open the curtain, a towel came through, it made me jump and I gave a little start.

"I'm sorry; I didn't mean to scare you." He held the towel out to me still. "Please." He sounded so nice and it was strange to be treated like this, I took it and when I stepped out of the shower I gave a small smile of appreciation. He had in his other hand a new night gown, he turned around whilst I dried myself and he handed me the dress. Once I had put it on, he turned back to me and placed the note in my hand.

"Keep it hidden until you get in your room. Read it then." He said barely above a whisper.

"But the cameras, he will see." I couldn't keep the fear from edging into my voice.

"Wait until you get in, go and sit on your bed with your back to the door, there is a blind spot there where the camera won't see your face or what is in front of you. But keep the note close and try to make it look as if you are looking out the window. He won't see."

"Are you sure he won't?" I asked him, scared and my voice wavering.

"Trust me Casey. Please. If you do, we might all get out of here alive." He took my hand and led me back to my room. Once I was inside and heard the door being locked behind me, I did what the kind stranger told me. I read the note and it simply said;

Help me please.
Jody Danvers

It was written in blood. In that moment, I realised what this was all for. In that moment, I realised what it was I had to do. I was the only one who could help. I had to find a way to free those poor girls trapped below, and if I could, save myself too.

JUNE 5TH 2017

It's been three days since my last entry and after the proceedings of the 2nd of June I spent that time in my room. Mostly in shock, but more importantly, entirely alone, the only time I had a visitor to my room was when food was passed through the door, so I'd spent my time sitting on my bed looking out the window, or lying on my bed, staring at the celling, trying to pass the time, the only thing I had to look forward to was the hand passing me food three times a day. It was only a small thing, but it was much more than I'd ever had before. I noticed it was the hand of the nice man and not my captor, which filled me with excitement, something I had experienced very little of.

Midday on the 3rd, I was looking out of my window, it overlooks the back garden, no other houses are visible and there was no way to see into the window unless from within the grounds itself, and if a stranger did make it into the grounds, then I doubt they would make it out, if they were stupid enough to try to but no-one ever was. All these years and never once have I heard a knock on the door. Looking out the window, there was a small shed not far from the back door. That day I saw something new, a man carrying large bags of something into the house, he made three trips and it wasn't until he came closer that I realised which man it was, the scar was clearly visible on his face.

After that nothing else happens until two days later, on the 5th, about midday again, I saw another man digging towards the back of the garden, hidden from view from everyone but me. I could see him well and he was wearing the classic jeans, white t-shirt and a blue base-ball cap. His lean, well-built body was visible as his shirt stuck to him with the sweat of exertion on such a hot day. He paused to take a drink of water, he took off his base-ball cap revealing long, chestnut brown hair, and turned towards the window, the distance was too far to see the expression on his face clearly, but I felt he was looking directly at me. The thought made me smile, and I didn't know why. I wondered what he was digging for.

That question was soon answered when, hours later, just before dusk I glimpsed him making his way from the house back towards the hole, this time though he wasn't alone, both men were there and they were both carrying something dark across the grass, my immediate guess was that it was the poor girl's body, still covered in the black sheet. 10 minutes later, the man I called scar returned to the house, before he reached the door, he stopped and looked up towards the window, towards me. He looked right at me. We held eye contact for a few minutes, and then he walked on into the house. The other man didn't return for another couple of hours. When he did, he wasn't walking straight, barely upright and stumbling all over the place, with a half empty bottle in his hand.

I went over to lie down on the bed; I put my arms behind my head and stared at the celling again. Only one thought entered my mind and that was about him. I remembered his body and the way the clothes showed that shape. I was just falling asleep when there was a gentle tapping at the door. I almost missed it but it happened a second time. I got up hesitantly, and made my way over to the door quietly, the tapping on the door came a third time. I put my ear to the door, trying to hear any sounds from the other side. I was afraid to open the door, but it was still locked from the outside so I didn't have much choice. I knew it wasn't Scar because he wouldn't knock. He'd just barge in. It must be the other one. His was sniffing, and mumbling to himself. I found the courage, and managed a weak "hello." The mumbling stopped and then he whispered back, slurring his words but they were still understandable,

"Will you let me in?" he asked, even in his drunk state he was gentle. I smiled, I couldn't help it,

"I can't. The door is locked from out there." I replied and there was a short silence.

"Oh", I let out a little giggle. Then I heard the jangle of keys as he searched for the right one to my door. He'd unlocked the door and was about to turn the handle when he stopped and asked again. "May I come in?" this time my hesitation wasn't out of fear but out of caution, locked away from the world I'd missed so much. I was so experienced in some ways, but in many ways, I was still ignorant, years behind my age. Boys, this topic was now presenting itself right on my doorstep, and I was about to invite a very attractive and, smoking hot boy into my room. This was foolish. I bit my lip.

"Yes" I replied and I stepped back from the door. He opened, entered, and closed it behind him. Then he did something unexpected and locked the door from inside. He must have seen my expression because he quickly added, "I've drugged the bastard, that mixed with the alcohol and he should be out for hours, but just in case, we don't want him barging in." He looked at the bottle in his hand, shook his head and looking disgusted with himself, he put the bottle down on the floor and made his way over to my bed and sat down. I had no other chairs in the room so unless I was going to sit on the floor or stand awkwardly, this was the only choice. But I felt safe around him though I did not know why. So, I went and sat beside him. I stayed quiet and waited for him to speak first. When he did, it was unexpected,

"I'm so sorry Casey." He put his face in his hands.

"For what?" I asked, curiously. He looked at me, and caringly stroked my cheek, I saw his eyes were red and they were starting to fill with tears.

"You're so beautiful." He said and let go of my face. The way he spoke, I might have only met him three days ago, but I had the feeling then that he'd known me for a lot longer.

"Do you remember anything about your life before you came here?"

"No, nothing really."

"Do you even remember how old you were? Do you know how old you are now?" I simply shock my head and he let out a sigh. In truth, I'd rather lost track of how long I'd been there, and in turn, how old I am. It's a terrible thought. I had found a battered and torn calendar out in the garden, one of the very rare times when I was allowed a supervised stroll around the gardens for fresh air; id seen the calendar on the floor by the trash, it had one day marked of so I took it to be the day before, and I've taken my dates from then. Whether I am correct, I do not know. For all I know the calendar is years old and I started from the wrong day! But having that helped, I had no connection to the outside world so whether I was syncing with them was irrelevant. The calendar, of course I hid under my mattress, along with this diary.

"You were 6 when he took you, and you are now 26. You've been here for 20 years." A silence grew. I didn't know what to say, twenty years. Wow!

"How long have you been here?" I asked him,

"20 years."

"20 years?! So, you've been here the same time as me?" he nodded.

"I'm so sorry Casey, I'm so, so sorry. I didn't want to; I had no choi-" he broke off mid-sentence. Instinctively I placed my hand comfortingly on his shoulder; I felt his whole body relax almost immediately.

"I was ten, when he took me. He did a job once with my father. My father messed up and cost the job dearly, he was a poor man and we didn't have money. Things were tough. Then Dimitri suggested taking me instead of the money. He said he could do with a strong lad to help him around the house and grounds. My parents couldn't afford my keep so they sent me with him that day. That night he gave me a job to do. I was to sneak into the home of a rich couple, the man owed Dimitri money for a job and refused to pay him as he claimed the job wasn't as agreed. Dimitri said they needed 'encouraging'. He made me steal their baby, their baby girl. If I refused, well. You saw the mess downstairs.

"Me?"

"Yes you, Casey. You catch on quick. I took you from your home and bought you to this hell."

"It wasn't your choice. The way I see it you had no choice."

"I could have died. No, the truth was I was scared and I took the cowardly path. I tried to take you back, a week later but he caught me. He locked you in here, kept me upstairs and made sure we never saw each other again. As punishment to me, he killed my family, and made me watch; my two sisters first, then my mother, then my father." He stopped now, biting his bottom lip. I held his hand and he squeezed mine. "Then whenever he went out I'd sneak down here, and sit outside your door. I tried to talk to you but you never replied. Often you were crying, so I'd hum to you, a tune my mum used to sing to me when I was afraid. That always calmed you."

"That was you!?"

"Yes, that was me."

"What's your name?" I asked him.

"I'm Shane. "

We sat there in a strange but happy silence; we were connected, from the start. This was why I felt so safe around him.

"Look, what happened the other day, the girl, in the kitchen. I want you to know, that wasn't me. He made us clear up the mess. But I'm done clearing up his mess. I don't want to do it anymore." His temper had started to rise, but it wasn't aimed at me, what he had done sickened him. Was this the only time he'd had to clean up messes like that? I was about to ask him but we heard boots stomping slowly up the stairs. We stood up quickly; he'd be at the top of the stairs by now. Then Shane turned to me, kissed me, and rushed out the door. He locked it just in time as Scar came to the top of the stairs; luckily, he'd been groggy and was looking down otherwise he'd have seen Shane coming out the door.

"What are you doing?" I heard him say.

"Nothing, I was just- "

"Move out of the way" he said and barged past him not taking notice of what he was saying. I heard the thump against the door as Shane was pushed against it. I heard the heavy footstep's going up to the attic; Shane hovered outside before following him.

I went to bed, tired and overwhelmed with everything Shane had told me, our history, my past. I was given a tiny snippet of it. Something solid. I felt worried for Shane but I managed to fall straight to sleep, and the most peaceful sleep I'd had for a very long time.

JUNE 6ᵀᴴ 2017

I woke up with a start that morning, I sat up on my bed, blinking furiously as understanding started to rein into my mind and I remembered the event of the night before. My thoughts fell straight to Shane and I wondered if he was all right, if he slept well, imagining me waking up beside him, his arm sprawled around my shoulders. I shook my head and I ran my hand over my face and rubbed my eyes, which then fell to the empty wine bottles Shane had left on the floor. I looked immediately up to the cameras in my room and my heart sank, my stomach began to do summersaults. What if Scar looked at the cameras? He would know Shane had been there talking to me and that would get us both into heaps of trouble. My fears were short lived though as I heard Shane call my name from the other side of the door; he opened the hatch and passed me a bowl of cereal.

"Casey, are you there?" I ran over to the door and crouched down beside the hatch. I took the bowl and brushed my hand against his, he started at my touch but he put the bowl on the floor and took my hand.

"Are you all right Shane, did he hurt you?"

"I'm fine Casey, don't worry about me, he didn't do anything I can't handle."

"Shane the cameras, he will see we were together last night, won't he?" he paused, as if wondering how he should reply.

"I thought about that last night, I think we will be fine. Scar hardly ever looks at the footage; he has no reason to, what with the locks on the doors."

"Oh" that seemed odd, how did Shane know that, and also, if that is true, then why did Shane tell me so specifically when and how to read the note to avoid the cameras?

"But, just in case he does decide to look, I'm going to sneak into the security room and erase the tapes, maybe damage the equipment so it looks like it's been down for a while, he won't know." I breathed a sigh of relief.

"And if you could damage one of the cameras too, that would be great." I'd asked before I comprehended I'd said it aloud. He let out a hearty laugh after hearing that.

"What?" I asked him, "I've never liked them, as if being here isn't bad enough I don't like being spied on 24/7."

"I knew I'd like you Casey, you have spirit." He tightened his grip on my hand. The door slammed upstairs and he quickly released his hold, slammed the hatch door shut and walked down the stairs.

Later that night Shane returned to my room, his knock on the door had urgency to it and I hurried over to the door to let him in. He burst in, his eyes alight with fury and he paced the room. I quickly closed the door and walked towards him, his pacing didn't cease so I followed him back and forth, asking him what was wrong but he didn't reply. He stopped pacing and let himself fall backwards on to the bed, his sigh held a lot of pain and despair. I was feeling something very strong for him, could this be love, is this what love felt like? I realised, when he fell backwards on to the bed, I saw his face that the possibility was high. You may think after only a week of a few encounters with him that I couldn't possibly love him. Maybe it was because we had both suffered something similar, both connected on our paths, paths that had, until now been running parallel with each other. Now, though, they crossed every so often. I only hoped they merged into one path that we could walk on together.

I went and lay down beside him. I felt so comfortable around him, it was as if I'd known him forever, and we'd been best friends. I had a feeling he felt the same about me too, but then he had known me a lot longer than I did him.

"We have to get out of here."

"Where is he now?" I asked him,

"Probably passed out in a ditch somewhere in the garden again. He's been drinking all day. The pressure is getting to him, he made a mistake on the last girl he snatched and I think they are close to finding him." he looked at me. Lying there beside me, I really didn't want him to leave.

"I decided to do some digging, and I found out a few things. One of the rooms downstairs, it's covered in pictures and photos of the latest girl. By the looks of it he'd been following her for weeks before he took her. He had all sorts of details about her, what routes she ran in the mornings, where she worked, and the coffee shop she went to. Things like that. But there were other folders in there too, very similar; there were over 20 folders there Casey, all of women, and children." He paused, and swallowed, his throat was going made as if he was going to be sick. "Some, he had drawn an 'X' right across the face, a red 'X'. There were only 7 girls whose photos weren't de-faced; you; the girl who died a few days ago, I guess he hasn't had time to delete her; 5 others and the one on the wall. Casey, including the new girl whose picture was on the wall, there are 6. 6 girls. 6 rooms. See where I'm going with this?" He sat up and I followed his movements as if attached by strings, I sat aghast at what I was hearing. 6 girls, there were 6 other girls down there. Then a thought came to me.

"Shane, their names, did you see their names on the folders?"

"I did but I don't remember them all, only their first names. There was Molly, Scarlet, Tara, Simone, Melany and Jody." He counted them on his fingers as he went through the list. At the last name I grabbed his arm.

"Jody Danvers?! Was that her name?"

"Possibly, it seems familiar but I'd need another look to be sure. Why?"

"Remember that note I found down in the cellar? It was from her, Jody Danvers."

"What did she say?"

"Help me please, was all the note said, but Shane, it was written in blood." He placed his hand on top of mine which was still holding his forearm. He didn't say anything, what could he say? Another thought then came to me.

"Shane, you said there were over 20 files, all of girls. What happened to the others?" Shane didn't look at me when I asked him that, he looked everywhere else except at me, got up and walked over to the window, he was upset and I got the impression he knew something and wasn't saying.

"Do you think he killed them, like he did that other poor girl?"

He stood staring out the window, I felt so sorry for him I joined him there. I saw he was crying.

"Oh Casey, I had no idea that's what they were. I swear."

"Woah, Shane slow down, what 'what' were?" I asked as he tried to slow his breathing.

"He'd always make me dig the holes. He'd put suitcases in the holes and made me bury them. They were heavy but I never assumed…" he cut off,

"You think he had bodies in the suitcase?"

"I didn't then no, I thought it was money or something, like a long-term deposit, so to speak. I never thought they were bodies. How could I be so stupid, but then I never saw the girls, I never saw him bring in new girls, for all I knew they were the same ones who'd been down there for years."

"How many?"

"How many what?"

"How many holes did you dig?"

"Over 20." He said weekly, we both knew now the likeliness of those suitcase now held the bones of helpless woman who died at the hands of a monster.

"When he forced me bury that poor girl's body like he did, only covered in a tarp, I should have put two and two together and seen the connection. But I didn't."

"It's not your fault Shane." I said to him, I took his face in my hand, the same way he did to me last night. "Like you said, you never saw the girls; you had no reason to suspect that he'd killed them, let alone hid their bodies in suitcase and make you bury them. It's not your fault." I was pleading with him to believe me. He sighed, and gave a weak smile. Then he did something so unexpected I was caught totally unawares. He pulled me close to him and held me tightly. He hugged me. I still remember his smell, a mix of sweet sweat and musky damp. His hair was so soft against my cheek. Then I did something even more surprising. I hugged him back, putting my arms around his waist and held him just as tightly. Then I kissed him gently on the cheek. He was surprised and stood back, but he smiled. Whether he smiled at the kiss or at my reaction when I realised I'd let my guard down and kissed him, I didn't know. But it was a smile that made me melt. He was still holding my hand, so that was a good sign right? He stood as if in thought, still looking at me. His look became enticingly puzzling, but I somehow knew what it meant, deep down. My stomach jumped and I suppressed a grin. I moved my mouth about to say something, but Shane stopped me,

"You don't need to say anything, I can see the subtle, loving look in your eyes, and I recognise it because it must equal what I am feeling." He paused; I knew he was thinking the same as I was. I turned from him as a typhoon of emotions washed over me. Could this really be? Could I really want him in that way, the buzzing in my body told me yes, but the memories of Scar flooded back and I didn't think I could do that with anyone else. I caught sight of him in the mirror, I'm embarrassed to say that I noticed he let his eyes fall to my bottom, he bit his lip, I could tell he just had to hold me, and if I was honest, I needed him to, now.

He stepped up behind me, gently grabbed my arm and turned me towards him. Breathing fast and smiling I mirrored his emotions, he couldn't contain it anymore. He pulled me to him and embraced me tightly, took my lips in his own, a warm, exciting passionate kiss as our tongues danced together. I was overtaken by the moment and forced him backwards, into the wall, accidently winding him, I managed a weak 'sorry' in between the kisses, breathlessly he returned a 'quite alright' and our union continued. Emotions were flooding through both of us. For me it was utter confusion, how could I be so desperate to have this man, any man after what I've been through, but at the same time I knew this could be different. Fear and excitement, I wanted to find out. Shane started to feel his excitement rising. I felt it too; it stirred butterflies through my stomach, followed by gentle tingling all over. Shane picked me up and I wrapped my legs around his waist, lips still entwined he blindly stepped forwards, all of his concentration was on me. He kissed my cheeks, made his way down my neck and settled on my collarbone where he nuzzled and suckled playfully, eliciting little moans and giggles from me.

Suddenly, tumbling backwards onto the bed, still holding me, we laughed as we landed on the soft mattress below. Lying in each other's arms, we momentarily stopped the kissing to catch our breath.

"Casey, look" he whispered gently into my ear, I followed his eye line out of the window, and the sky was slowly turning to dusk. As the last red glow from the setting sun came shining through the window, the earliest stars began to twinkle afar in a beautiful haze of soothing colours. We looked at each other, grinning from ear to ear.

"Casey, would it be it odd if, given our short acquaintance I told you I've fallen for you?" I smiled shyly,

"I don't think it would be because, given our short acquaintance, I think I've fallen for you too."

I kissed his ear, he held me closer.
I nibbled his earlobe, he gripped my bottom.
I kissed his neck, his cheek and his lips.
He couldn't help smiling.
I kissed his forehead, his nose, and his lips again. Pure relaxation spread through my body, I looked him in the eyes again and he held my gaze. I moved my kisses down to his chin, my wet lips moved against the hollow of his throat. I slipped my hands under his shirt, feeling the warmth of his body under my body; my skin erupted with hundreds of

emotions. I slipped his jumper up, that cute, white t-shirt he wore so well, so sexy. Now I wanted him out of it and he was, it was on the floor beside us. I returned to the exploration of his torso, planting kisses on every inch I could find as I made my way still lower, my lips hit his belt. Yet another obstacle. I un-notched the belt, undid the button. Kiss. The zip, slowly the zip came down. He lifted his pelvis slightly so I could remove the final obstacle. His pants and underpants were now lying beside us too. Then I froze.

"No" Shane said, breathing heavily as he reached down and gently held me by my chin and pulled my face to his, "Don't do that. Don't do what he made you do. Not to me." I was still rigid, and he could sense my tension. "I want you to enjoy this, remember this and love us. Not to fear it, and hate it. With the right person, it is something amazing and magical. Let me show you. Trust me, try and relax." He span me round so he was now on top, and sliding his hand along my inner thigh, his fingers brushed against me, eliciting a little excited 'oh' from me. He continued to move his hand along the contours of my body, he gently gripped and massaged my breast, feeling them harden in his palm. My clean nightgown now lay crumpled atop his clothes as we were both now naked and free to the elements of that warm night. He slowly moved my legs apart and entered, still sharing a passionate kiss. His speed slowly increased to match the soft sounds now emanating from me. This was different, he was so gentle, I could not believe it possible. I clung, accidently digging my fingertips into the nape of his back, I pulled him even closer, I could feel the pressure of his body on top of me, but this time it wasn't suffocating, it was comforting, I felt safe and I never wanted it to stop. I wrapped my legs around him, my muscles tightened and I arched my back, my body convulsed as I reached that point of pure pleasure, normally it would be over by now, he'd be pulling his jeans on, and walking out the room, not a word said. I would be lying still barely wanting to breathe. But this, this was, there were no words to describe.   His breathing intensified as did mine and we began kissing any part of each other we could, in that moment, reach.

Time seemed to slow, we shared a special moment, conjoined as one body, our breathing and movements became one, in perfect harmony we danced to the music of our beating hearts. Every part of our bodies hummed and buzzed pleasantly as we remained one. We lived what felt a lifetime of happiness in that one soaring perfection.
Breathing heavily, excitedly, passionately, Shane collapsed gently, applying the full weight of his body onto me and nuzzled my cheek. My hot breath released into his ear as I breathed, released shivers spiraling down his spine. We lay there in this moment together, Shane still comfortably inside me, neither giving signs that we wanted this to change, our breathing, as one, slowed. Shane looked at me, the euphoria twinkled in his eyes and I'm sure my emotions ran across my face. We smiled at each other and laughed at the pure happiness eradiating through every inch of our naked bodies as we lay in the now damp and sweaty bed sheets. Shane, reluctantly moved to lie beside me, I turned and placed my head on his chest as he placed his arm around my shoulder. My pent-up emotions and silent desires of the past years, to know if this intimacy of this kind could be any different from what I had experienced with Scar was finally allowed gratification and it was far from disappointing, it was elating and electrifying, still buzzing as our skin tingled in the aftermath of our ecstasy. We lay there like that for what felt like hours, blissful, peaceful, happy, and fear-free. I didn't want him to ever leave my room. We heard clanging and breaking downstairs which aroused both of us from our sleepless slumber, we hurriedly, but playfully dressed each other, still giggling happily. I walked with him over to the door and we kissed again in a very reluctant parting, we had to be quiet and hope he wouldn't hear Shane leaving my room. It seemed that whenever we parted, it was always in hope he hadn't seen us together and I really looked forward to a time in the future when we wouldn't have to. Could that

ever really be? I hope so, but at least, for now, I have the memories of tonight to keep me through.

JUNE 7TH 2017

The following day Shane returned to my room mid-morning, he tapped on the door and I was getting used to recognising when it was him on the other side of the door and Scar hadn't visited my room in a few nights, (but after the escapades with Shane last night I hoped however I had many more nightly visits from Shane.) I felt certain it was Shane. I was getting quite relaxed in my surroundings, the anxiousness I felt whenever I heard a floor board creak or the groan of an old door hinge as it allowed a servant of the beast to enter across its threshold, dwindle since being with Shane. He barely waited until I'd fully opened it before he pulled me into the corridor, kissed me on the lips and gripped me tightly.
"Good morning" I said happily when he loosened his hold.
    "I couldn't stop thinking about you all night." He whispered and I melted.
    "Nor I, you." He grabbed my wrist and started to lead me down the corridor.
    "Shane! Wait, you're hurting my wrist" He stopped abruptly,
    "I'm sorry" he kissed my hand. "We don't have long but there's something you have to see." He took my hand this time holding it firmly but not roughly and I walked slightly behind him, the corridor was too narrow for two to walk aside each other.
    "Where is Scar?"
    "Who?" he asked puzzled but he didn't stop walking.

"Scar, where is he, has he gone?"

"Oh. You're telling me you don't even know his name, after all these years?"

"We didn't exactly stop to chat you know. He never told me, I never asked."

"His name is Dimitri." And not another word was said between us until we made it down to the cellar. We stopped just at the top of the stairs, there was a very small landing and a door just to the left which I'd completely missed the only other times I'd passed it not blindfolded, the first when Dimitri dragged me up the stairs and the second when he threw me down them only a few days ago.

Shane stopped, checked the back window from where he stood then took a key from his pocket. The door had a small lock and the key stuck a little. It took a little bit of shimmying it to finally get it to open, which it did into a very small study. On the wall was one screen, and on it were three different views of my bedroom, clearly visible. I followed the lines of dust and cobwebs that hung down from the ceiling. I doubted the room had ever been cleaned. Then I saw the wall Shane had mentioned previously, pictures of a girl, pretty. Very pretty. In her late teens, she had dark brown hair and eyes to match. She had a lovely smile and I could see why someone like Dimitri would take a liking to her, and there was her name, Jody Danvers.

Shane pointed out the stack of folders, 6 in all. He started sifting through them looking for something. I went over to the taller stack of folders which were covered in a light layer of dust, disturbed only by a hand print which I took to be Shane's. Then something caught my eye; above the desk there was a picture hanging on the wall, the picture itself wasn't viewable under the thick coating of dust but there was a mark just to the left of the painting as if something had been scraped against it, like a picture frame. The picture was hanging slightly to the right. I nudged the frame further to the right and it revealed a small cupboard, not locked luckily.

"Shane, over here." he looked up and put the folder he was holding back on the stack. "Check this out." I pointed to the secret cupboard. He opened the door and took out four folders.

They were of boys, each one no older than 8 or 9. On the inside of each folder was a few words scrawled in an elegant hand. Shane read the first one. 'Not much hope for this one, too feisty. He has to go." He looked and me and turned the page to reveal a picture, a big red cross against the boy's face. He handed me that folder and looked at the next. 'Disappointing, there was hope until he befriended one of the brats. He had to go.' We held our breath as he turned the page over, red starred at us. He hastily opened the next one; this simply said 'disposed of.' I felt very sick and there was the blood red 'x'. I had to look away and brought my hand to my mouth. I didn't look at the next picture but I heard Shane slowly shuffle through the papers of the next folder.

"Oh my God." He exclaimed beside me, my curiosity got the better of me and I glanced at the pages.

"Oh my God" I repeated and there on the page was a picture of a young boy, dark black hair, brown eyes and across his cheek and lip was the tell-tale large scar, unmistakable scar. Underneath was a name, Dimitri Ustranov. Shane turned to the front of the folder and there was written; 'a very hopeful young boy. He has guts, doesn't say much but does as told with little fight. Perfect. I will make him my apprentice.'

We both stood dumbfounded at what we had read. So, our captor was a victim himself. Taken, like us, as a child and trained to kill. Who'd have thought! But who was his captor? There was no description in the folder. Who was he? Shane put the folders back in the secret cupboard and just as he was about to close it noticed that the back of the cupboard had a latch. The secret cupboard had a secret hub. He took the folders back out and pulled the latch which revealed another, slightly thinner folder. Shane's hands began to shake as he removed it. He handed me the folder and told me he couldn't look anymore, so I took a deep breath and hesitantly took the folder from him, he stood beside me as I slowly opened the page, we didn't know what to expect but what we found had sickened us more than anything else. The folder contained many sheets of paper, all with a picture of one of the girls and a picture of a baby, birth details and account details. From the look of the information here the poor women he kept downstairs he raped, made them pregnant and their children taken from them most likely immediately after birth and sold, for a handsome sum. There's no way this was legal. It couldn't possibly be. If he had all that money, where was it? It certainly wasn't put into the house. We didn't say a word, I put the folders back, Shane returned the picture and I nudged it back to how it was, leaning slightly to the right. Hopefully Dimitri wouldn't notice the unwelcomed guest the next time he was down here. We took one last look around the room and confident that everything looked undisturbed we went out, the door squeaking shut behind us. As Shane was trying to lock the door with the same difficulty he had in opening it, I took a chance and went slowly down the stairs. By the time I reached the bottom Shane had looked my way and ran down behind me.

"No, Casey. What are you doing?!" he exclaimed, horror and fear came over his voice.

"We can't leave them down here! After what we've just read?! He is a trained killer and a nutcase, I am not leaving them down here to be raped anymore, and how many of them are already pregnant?" I struggled against his grip.

"No Casey. We can't! Not now, not like this. If we do this on impulse, it will get us all killed, we'll all end up lying in our own pool of blood. He became urgent and desperate but he spoke the truth and I knew it. It would be silly to try a rescue with no plans. I reluctantly nodded and he released my arm, I looked back at the doors and my heart sank. I hoped the girls were still alive. I followed him up the stairs to the kitchen, he stopped and nodded to the table, I sat down nervously. I'd never been in this room for longer than a few minutes. Shane went over to the kettle and turned it on, neither of us spoke and the sound of the steam bellowing from the hole drowned out the awkward silence. He poured us two cups of coffee and took a seat opposite me. The steam of our coffees came between us. I realised my earlier statement of 'servant of the beast' was a little harsh for Dimitri, he was made this way, created to be a killer. I almost felt sorry for him. Almost. We were so engrossed in our own thoughts that we didn't hear the car door slam shut on the driveway.

"GO!" Shane shouted as footsteps were crunching on the gravel path. I didn't need telling twice, I bolted out the kitchen and up the stairs. It was only when I got to the second floor that I realised Shane still had the key, my door locked itself when shut and required a key to open it from this side, I was stuck out here on the landing. It was too late, I heard the back door open and the flow of conversation, but it was too quiet to hear any words. That didn't last long though,

"WHO WERE YOU TALKING TO?" Dimitri belted his Russian accent stronger and slurred from alcohol. He was drunk again. I heard a scraping of chairs and cups smashing. I hovered at the top of the stairs, would I cause more trouble if I went downstairs? I decided I was better off waiting up here, for both me and Shane's sakes. Shane mumbled something inaudible then I heard loud footsteps stomping up the stairs, he was heading this way. Shane's lighter steps were close behind.

"I'm going to kill her." He said roughly.

"CASEY RUN!" Shane shouted up from further down the stairs. I tried to run but sudden panic rooted my feet to the spot. I saw the top of his head coming up the stairs as he used his hands to pull himself up the last few. Finally, I turned to run, but it was too late, he dived forwards and grabbed my ankle tripping me and pulling me down, my face smashed into the floor and I felt a hot liquid running over my lips. I tried to take a breath and spluttered blood all over the floor. He turned me round and tried to pull me closer. By that time, Shane had made it up the stairs and grabbed Dimitri by the hair and off me; Dimitri swung round and caught Shane in the head with the bottle still in his hand. Shane staggered back and slumped against the wall. He didn't move. A small bead of blood began to run down the side of his head. Dimitri turned back to me, grabbed me by the hair and fumbled to get the key out of his pocket and into the lock. He flung the door open; a loud dull thud came as the handle hit the wall. Another dull thud came as he pushed me through the door and I hit the floor, two more thuds happened as his fist contacted my face. My eyes blurred, and my face now coated in blood I found it hard to see or breath. He picked up my head and thumped it back against the floor.

What happened next I didn't remember but when I woke I was cold, the blood had dried on my face and hair; my pants and clothes were heaped in the corner of the room. I struggled to get up and dragged the sheets off the bed in an attempt to get up on it. I forced myself up, my body covered in bruises, my head spinning I felt so sick that I keeled back over and threw up on the floor. Exhausted I slumped onto the bed. It was dark outside. The room was spinning as I closed my eyes and fell into a fitful sleep.

JUNE 8TH 2017

When I woke up I was so stiff from the beating I'd received that I had to move very slowly. It took me far longer to get up from the bed; I barely made it to the bathroom in time. Dimitri had installed a toilet and a small sink in the corner of my room a few years ago, when he got fed up with having to keep coming up here to let me out. He put up a small curtain that gave me a miniscule bit of privacy. You get used to it. The act of relieving myself was a task in its self, the pain was immense, he'd been very rough with me on last night's attack, I'm glad I couldn't recall it. I didn't dare sit for a while so I gently leant against the window and looked out. The sun was high in the sky, it was well past morning. I was surprised Shane hadn't come to see if was ok. Unless he couldn't and took a fair beating himself. As I looked out the window my worries were cleared, I saw Dimitri and Shane walking down the gravel path to the car. They were going out. Dimitri was walking with a slight limp; he must have hurt himself in his drunken state. There were no tell-tale signs of Shane being badly injured, although I couldn't see his face, but he wasn't limping. I felt relieved.

    I stood there looking out for as long as my legs would allow me, the sky was still light, but turning darker. They still hadn't returned. I took a chance and slowly edged my way over to the bed and very slowly lowered myself down, I managed to get into a fairly comfortable position and closed my eyes.

It wasn't long afterwards that I heard three car doors slamming and low, quiet arguing. I rushed over to the window far quicker than I should have and I had to steady myself for a moment. When I looked at the window I saw two men and a shape lying on the ground. The two men were arguing, the bundle on the floor was not moving. I think I made out a hand behind the tire. Something didn't seem right; I edged over to the wall and hid myself behind the curtain, peering out behind it. No bottles were in anyone's hand, this wasn't a drunken chaos; this was real panic. Something had gone seriously wrong. Then Shane hoisted the bundle over his shoulder and headed off towards the back garden. It was then that I saw what he was carrying, it was another girl. Dimitri bent down and picked something else up off the grass, it was a knife. I was afraid with what I'd seen so I rushed over to my bed and lay down. I wanted so badly to feel the comforting hold of Shane's warm arms, but at the same time I was hoping beyond all hope that neither Shane nor Dimitri visited my room that night. Something didn't feel right and in the passing hours I swirled all ideas and thoughts around my mind, working myself up considerably. That night consisted of the worse night's sleep I'd had since my childhood years.

JUNE 9TH 2017

I woke up very hungry that morning, I'd been in too much pain the day before to realise that I hadn't eaten and no-one had come up to give me any food either. I lay still on the bed for a few minutes; there was complete silence, no boot sounds, no crunching gravel, and no creaking doors. Nothing. Was I along again today as well? I wondered where Shane and Dimitri were today, and then I found my thoughts travelled back to Shane and his strong hands, his warm body and luscious lips. I spent all last night worrying, the most insane things came into my mind, that Shane wasn't who he said he was, but once I'd calmed down, I'd realised it was just my eyes playing tricks on me. Shane was annoyed that he was burying yet another body, Dimitri ordering him like he always does.

I spent most of that morning wishing Shane would come and speak to me. I missed his voice and his smile. There was a loud, frantic knock at the front door, which even up here on the third floor was fully heard. All my time here and I'd never heard an attack on the door like that before, I was suddenly overcome with curiosity and I rushed to my door, I got down on the floor, with great difficulty and opened the hatch, I put my ear as close to it as possible trying to hear anything of the conversation below. I held my breath to take away all noise I could. Still I heard nothing, I was too far away. I went over to the window and strained to see the door right underneath my window. All I could make out was three male heads. After five minutes, they turned from the door and headed away. Then I noticed their clothing, the man in the middle was wearing a smart black suit with a white shirt, but it was the other two men that made my heart flutter, they were officers. The police were at the door. But they were walking away, I had one chance, I started banging on the window, waving, anything to get them to notice me. But they didn't look up. They were almost out of sight when the door flung open and I felt two arms grab me from behind and drag me to the floor. I'd been banging on the window loud enough to draw attention from inside the house. I screamed out for help but he pushed his hand over my mouth and silenced me. I fought back as best I could, pain now vibrated all over my body, the bruises being pounded on again by the weight of his body above me.

"They won't save you, girl. No-one will." I got my hand free and hit him on the chin, but it was weak and did nothing but provoke him. "You'd better get used to this, because this is all you will ever know." Then he hit me, first in the stomach and again. Then in the ribs. Pound, pound, pound. I felt a crack, breathing became hard. Then he hit me in the face. Hard. Hard enough that I blacked out.

JUNE 10TH 2017

I woke up with the soft mattress below and the comfort of the sheet above. I'd taken two big beatings in two days which left me physically and emotionally exhausted, I didn't want to do anything, I didn't even have the energy to get up nor did I want to attempt it, what was the point? Like Dimitri said, 'this is all I'll ever know' so I might as well get used to it. So I closed my eyes and fell back to sleep. How long I was like that for I couldn't tell. But I didn't care. The fight that had so rapidly sparked up within me to escape and live had dissipated just as quickly and I didn't care. I cried myself to sleep multiple times that day.

JUNE 11ᵀᴴ 2017

I felt so weak; I didn't want to sit up. Shane was sitting on the bed beside me; he held a bowl of something in his hand. I saw his lips moving but my mind didn't register what he was saying. Slowly I came round and heard him pleading me to eat something,

"Come on Casey, you've not eaten for days. You're weak. Here, have a little food." I didn't reply, I just shook my head and turned away from him. He sighed, put the bowl on the bedside table and left. I heard the lock click and a tear rolled down my cheek. I fell asleep.

JUNE 12TH 2017

It was evening when I finally woke up. Shane must have paid me another visit as there was a fresh bowl of soup on the table beside me. The sleep had renewed a little strength and given my injuries a chance to heal. If only a little. The soup smelled so good it enticed me to have some, I suddenly realised just how hungry I was. I tucked in and devoured the soup in minutes. It had cooled on the side and was just warm enough to heat my insides but not cause pain by the speed I ate it. I put the bowl back on the side and tried to get up, my legs were weak from limited movement in the last few days, my bones were stiff and muscles weak. I wondered then what had been happening while I'd slept but I instantly squashed out those thoughts. Dimitri was right, I had to accept this was my life; I didn't want another beating for interfering. I heard car doors close again but this time I didn't go over and look. I was determined not to look. I didn't want to know. It seemed however, that the universe had other ideas and wouldn't allow me to stay out of it. I heard a girl's voice, a call for help. I nervously edged to the window and saw Dimitri dragging a girl across the grass by her hair, she'd been gagged so she couldn't call out again but she wasn't going easily, I'd never seen a girl fight like that, resisting like she did. She looked up at the window and caught my eyes. When she saw me her eyes widened. I stepped back from the window, confused and torn between wanting to help her and wanting to save myself. I heard loud smashing and crashes come from below. She'd broken free of his grip and was trying to get away, then the cellar door opened and closed and all was silent. I heard the car door close again and the engine start. The gravel crunched as it drove away.

I crouched down in the corner and began to cry, I didn't know what to do. I froze as I heard the light click of the door, as the lock was opened. I shivered at the thought of Dimitri paying me another visit. I waited, but the door didn't open. Instead a small piece of white paper appeared under the door. I picked it up and read it. All it said was;

'Save them if you can.'

Save who? The girls? Why did Shane think I could save them and why didn't he say anything to me. Why didn't he tell me himself and help me, like he said he would? Had he found a plan? Or maybe he couldn't. I tried the handle and the door popped open. Still kneeling on the floor I poked my head out and had a look in the corridor. It was clear, I listened intently for any noise, but there was none. I was too afraid, I closed the door and went back to my bed and climbed under the covers. Shane had given me a chance to save them, or a chance to run and save myself. I cried as I thought about how the latter option was swaying my mind. I feared I wouldn't save the girls and I knew I would never forgive myself if I escaped and didn't try to save them. In that moment, I did the only thing I felt I was capable of and that was to choose neither, if I stayed in my room long enough maybe it would all just pass me by.

JUNE 15TH 2017

Over those three days I did all I could to ignore the possibility of having turned down my only chance of getting away. I didn't allow myself to feel that I'd made a very big mistake. I couldn't go down that path. I slept, I used the toilet, and I ate the food that was left at my door. No visitors. After three days, I started to regain my strength, my spirit, which, although still greatly diminished, wasn't destroyed.

JUNE 16TH 2017

Today, everything changed. I went over to the door to pick up the bowl of food. As I picked it up I noticed that it was just cereal in the bowl, no milk. Which was odd. I noticed that there was a small, white triangle poking out between the flakes. I ruffled through the flakes and found a piece of paper folded multiple times. I unfolded it slowly trying not to damage it. By now I no longer cared about the cameras. He already knew I'd been talking to Shane, no doubt seen our night of passion, so I didn't hesitate in opening the note where I stood. It was written in an elegant, narrow script. The message read:

> *'The girls need your help. Tonight.*
> *Go to the second room on the first floor,*
> *The keys to their doors will be on the desk.*
> *Your door will be unlocked and no-one will be here.*
> *The police know, they have people outside waiting.*
> *Get them out and past the boundary walls and they will meet you*
> *And you will be safe.*
> *Don't be afraid, you must trust me.*
> *S*

It was signed with an 'S', it was Shane! Shane had a plan and he needed my help. But could I do it? I had until the night time to decide whether I was strong enough. I had mere hours to decide the future of myself and the girls below. The pressure grew and the decision became harder and harder as the time ticked closer.

*****

Night had fallen. I heard footsteps out on the corridor, they stopped outside my door and I heard the key in the lock. The footsteps carried on and down the stairs. The door closed and the gravel crunched under foot. A car engine started and the car took off down the drive. This was the moment. It was now or never. I paced around the room for a minute or so, undecided, anxiety edged into my entire body and I started shaking uncontrollably. Then I found myself charging out the door before I had a chance to change my mind. My breathing got heavy and panic kicked in. I went very slowly towards the top of the stairs, taking one step at a time as I went down, the first floor was clear, I walked up to the second door and my hand on the handle I paused, what if the note was a trick? I was so quick to believe it was Shane, but what if it wasn't and this was a trap. What if I opened the door and Scar was standing there. If I went back to my room, maybe he'd be easy on me? "NO!" I shouted to myself, it made me jump and shook me out of my thoughts. "I've come too far now. Trust him Shane said. I have to trust him. You can do this." I nodded to myself and opened the door and without looking around I ran to the desk and grabbed the keys off the desk. They were exactly where he told me they would be. So far, he had been true.

I continued down to the kitchen with no interruptions. I rushed to the cellar door but it took me a while to find the right key because they all looked similar but finally I found the right one. Standing on the top of the stairs I looked down into the cellar, it was dark, darker than usual and I was afraid to go down there, I had a strong feeling that if I did, I might not be coming back up again, at least not alive.

I was shaking all over and barely standing upright. I took one step down and my legs gave way, I fell the rest of the way and landed with a groan. I started to cry, the pain was unbearable. I'd clearly made quite a noise because I heard a faint banging coming from inside one of the cells. I remembered my time in that room very little. One thing though that I do remember vividly however was the solid walls, they blocked out all noise so whoever was banging loud enough for me to hear it out here must either have some sort of pole or her hands must be very banged up. I started at the first door, trying each key until I found the correct one. Behind door number one was a girl I recognised as Molly Havers. She was cowering in the corner, her courage failed when the door had opened. Her hands were red and covered in blood; her knuckles were ripped and bloodied from where she'd been rapping hard against the walls. I went in to her, clutching my side, the broken rib causing me trouble after the fall. She remained cowering in the corner when I rushed over to her; she turned away from me as I got close. It took a lot of convincing her I was here to help her and eventually the beaten look and bruises I had on view must have changed her mind, she held out a hand and I helped her up. She was shaking, but didn't say anything so I handed her some keys,

"Here take these, try all the doors hurry!" I took her hand and ran out the door but she pulled her hand from mine as she came to the threshold. I stopped and looked back to her. She hesitated and looked towards the cellar door and then back to me. "He is not here but we don't have much time." She tiptoed out behind me and went to the next door, we tried the doors in order, my keys first and if they were unsuccessful she would try hers and soon enough we had five doors open and five girls were standing behind me, huddled together in a small group. They were looking at the last door; this door gave me the shivers. It was the same door behind which held the horror of the dead girl's blood, I dreaded what I would find behind that door, but so far five girls were still alive behind me, and I had to hope this girl would be too. I unlocked the door and slowly swung it open, I barely had time to step in before a body lunged at me and knocked me down, her fist hit my face a few times but I didn't fight back, in time she stopped and got off me. She looked at me, and then to the other girls huddled together then back to me and tears ran down her face as she walked towards me and helped me up.

"I'm sorry." She said shakily, "I thought it would be him again."

"It's ok." I took a deep breath as I tried to get up; she patted my shoulder as I did.

"Let's go." I said and headed towards the stairs but no one behind me moved, they were looking up into the door way, I turned my back on the door and went towards them. "Come on. All we have to do is get past the boundaries and we are safe, the police are waiting for us but we have to go now!"

"How do you know?" one of the girls asked,

"We don't have time, come on." I said desperately

"What if it's a trap?" one of them said to the other,

"How can we trust her?" Said another one, they stepped away from me as if I was contagious. I took a small step forward, anger began to grow inside.

"I've risked my life to come down here and get you out. If you'd rather go back to your cells and wait for someone else to come and save you, by all means do." I folded my arms and stood to the side, giving them the option. It seemed to work, they began to move forward, but they stopped at the bottom of the stairs and looked towards me, it looks like I'd be going first. The pain I'd gone through in the last few days, the added beating by the girl and they distrust I'd received from them all had fueled the anger and, I suppose a good thing, it overpowered the fear and I grumbled as I barged ahead of them and up the stairs. I stopped at the top and listened, I couldn't hear anything so I ushered the girls up and toward the back door. It was only a short distance and I could see the gates and there were men just behind it, the police. I told them to run for the gates, we started running, I bringing up the rear, slower than the rest because of all my injuries. The other girls seemed to have been invigorated by their sudden freedom and ran like the wind.

That was when we heard it, two gun shots echoed through the air, the girls screamed and I saw the girl in front of me fall face down, the other girls screaming continued, I paused and could hear the police yelling at us to run. Out from behind the dustbins emerged a hooded male figure, he had his back to me and was slowly reloading the shot gun, either he hadn't seen me or wasn't worried about me for the time being. He aimed the gun and shot again towards the girls. They turned and ran, luckily, they had made it to the gates, he fired the shots but missed any and all targets, by intent or accident, it wasn't clear. I saw they were safe when the final girl was scooped into the arms of a waiting police man who rushed her out of harm's way, when suddenly a hand came from behind me and clamped over my mouth, I was roughly pulled backwards and dragged back into the house.

"SShhhh" he kept whispering to me. I had one chance of freedom that day and I'd failed, five girls were free. One was lying dead on the grass outside and here I was being dragged right back up the stairs and into the room I was so close to never having to return to. He pushed me through the door, still holding me so I didn't fall and closed the door behind him and to my surprise locked it.

"Shane, what are you playing at?! We could have run. We could have been free." I said, scared and frustrated. He went straight to the window, still behind me; he took me over there too. "Shane, Wha-"he'd released his grip and I'd turned round to face him; to my utter shock, I was not looking into the face of Shane, instead Dimitri stood there, ignoring me, looking out the window.

The police started shooting and made the hooded man retreated back behind the dustbins. Dimitri moved toward me but stopped as I stepped back and tripped over the bed. He saw the horror on my face and saw my mouth open but he was on top of me faster than I could make a sound, his hand went straight to my mouth, again. Not. Anymore. This time, I bit his finger and he let out a pained squawk but he only pressed down firmer.

"Shhhhhh, sshhhhhh." There was pleading in his voice, not command and malice. My eyes widened, "If I let you go, you have to promise me you'll listen. You don't understand." His accent was strong and panicked. His eyes, I saw, held as much fear as I knew he saw in mine. "Do you promise?" I nodded. He removed his hand but didn't get up immediately, I did nothing. He rolled off me and sat on the bed next to me. I was still lying still, in shock. I thought he was the one with the gun downstairs. Then it hit me. If he was up here, and not Shane, then where was Shane? Had he killed him? And who, if it wasn't Dimitri, was the man downstairs? Something about his manner made me feel the earlier wasn't true, this didn't seem like a man who had just killed his apprentice. He was shaking more than I was. I slowly sat up beside him. My eyes never left his beaten and unshaven face. I followed the side of his face to where there was blood dripping from his left ear, a large gash above his left eyebrow, and two rows of scratches on his left cheek. Fresh blood was dripping over dried blood. It was a mess and as I moved further round I could see his face was also wet from tears, he was crying. I had no idea what was happening right now, I couldn't fathom how this monster of a man who had beaten me and abused me since I was a child was now sitting beside me covered in blood, crying. Suddenly, he broke down, his face in his hands he sobbed quietly. I noticed his hands, also covered in slashes and cuts which went up his arms. He'd clearly been in a fight with a knife. I sat there with no idea what I should do, but pity came over me. There was something else gnawing away at my insides but I didn't want to pay attention to it. I got up, the sudden movement made him jerk and he looked up at me as if he'd forgotten I was there. His eyes widened. My jaw clenched but neither of us moved. We looked into each other's eyes, and with an unspoken understanding between us I moved towards the sink, grabbed a bowl from underneath and picked up the shirt that was lying on my floor. I took both back over to the bed; Dimitri never took his eyes off me all the while. I sat beside him, dipped the shirt in to the bowl and began to clean up his face. He flinched at the first few touches, and then he settled down. The look in his eyes turned to disbelief. He slowly moved his hand toward my hand and held it. I flinched at his touch, as he did with mine. But I didn't move it away, I couldn't, the fear I'd always known when around him kicked in.

"Why are you helping me like this?" he said, "After everything I did to you?"

I didn't answer, what could I answer? I just simply carried on cleaning him up the best I could but I had nothing to bandage his cuts with. I paused, watching him. His face showed a softness I'd never noticed before, we'd never been in the same room together when I wasn't cowering somewhere in fear or knocked unconscious. I can't explain it to you, but it was as if the past had shifted, we were living now in the moment and not the past. He'd saved me and I'd helped him, as if we were suddenly on the same side of a battle, but who was now the enemy? He was shaking; I helped him lie down on my bed, took the blanket off the end of the bed and covered him with it. He settled into it and closed his eyes. I went over to the window and took up my normal position of watcher. I kept one eye on him. I might have found a small bit of pity for him, but I certainly didn't trust him.

*****

The gun shots had silenced, the police had grown in numbers and now had the grounds surrounded. The blue lights were flashing brightly through the trees and illuminated the room. Dimitri groaned and joined me by the window.

"Not long now." He said. "We just have to survive one more night. Maybe two." He moved me away from the window.

"What do you mean?"

"The police, they will save us." Although his accent was strong, his English was very good.

"I don't understand. Where's Shane? Is he all right?"

"Humph. Still you care about that rat. Don't you realise?"

"Realise what?" I asked through gritted teeth, dread leaked into my heart.

"Shane, he is not who you think him to be. No doubt he showed you that file of me down in the cellar room?" my mouth fell open. He smirked, there it was, that same smirk I knew so well on that face, just minus the malice in his eyes, it wasn't as frightening.

"You know about that, how?" I asked shakily, he shook his head.

"I'm guessing he told you I'd claimed him as payment from his father? That I forced him to kidnap you, as initiation? That he'd been treated like you, kept separate from you because I thought he was getting too close?" I didn't answer, I didn't have to; my face apparently said it all. "He does that with them all, gains their trust. He makes out he loves them and treats them to a night of passion to make them love him back, that usually leads to their deaths. You were lucky Casey. Very lucky, you are different to him. Special. I have watched him watch you all these years. He is fascinated with you, Casey." He said my name so gently, tears filled my eyes, overwhelmed with what he was telling me I had no idea who or what to believe, I hated him. I didn't want to believe him. Shane wouldn't do that, he just wouldn't. My anger erupted,

"YOU LIAR! TELL THE TRUTH. SHANE WOULDN'T DO THAT." I spat, and hit him multiple times; he didn't fight me back, or try to stop me like I knew he could. He just stood there, taking the hits. After a few minutes, my anger slowed and I ceased hitting him.

"Why don't you fight back," I spat at him.

"I deserve it and more."

"What?" wha-"

"You have no reason to trust me bu-"

"Damn straight I don't."

"Please, just think about it." He pleaded, I thought.

"I don't understand? Think about what? How am I Lucky?" these questions and more flooded through my mind. "He was going to kill me?" I said more to myself in disbelief.

"Yes." Tears filled his eyes, he moved beside me and touched my cheek trying to comfort me but I pushed his hand away and stood up.

"Don't touch me." I spat, with more venom then I intended. He looked like I'd punched him in the stomach, but he didn't get up. He just sat there. "Explain. And start from the beginning."

"He showed you the folder of my captor? Did you see the picture of him?"

"There was no picture of him."

"That's because Shane didn't want you to know who he really is Casey. What he really is. He is the monster Casey, he kidnapped me. Took me from my family and brought me here, he took my sister too and kept her in his other house, my parents he killed."

"Other house?"

"Yes, he owns several houses, like this one where the cellar and the grounds hold many dark secrets." My stomach dropped.

"The babies."

"Yes."

"So, the children are his."

"No, he never did the...." He stopped mid-sentence and cleared his throat. "No, they are mine, mostly; he just dealt with the sales. It was Shane that forced me to do those things to you; he wanted me to do them. All those nights, he was watching us in that little room. He enjoyed seeing you in pain at the hands of someone else, it turned him on knowing you were vulnerable, and the more I put you through, the easier it would be for him to control you. He merely waited until he was ready and you were." My mind wouldn't comprehend what he was telling me, there were too many years, too many painful memories for Dimitri not to be the monster and the possibility that put my faith, my love in the wrong man, and I couldn't fathom that, not at the moment.

"Your hands and face, the bruises and cuts, Dimitri, was that Shane?"

"Yes, it was."

"What happened?" he seemed hesitant to tell me, but I was getting intrigued and irritated, things were starting to fall into place; things you don't see as vital in the moment, but when you look back on them years later, with a new perspective and new information they all make sense. I wanted to know the truth; he seemed the only one able to give me that now. He just seemed relieved he could finally tell someone the truth.

"We went out looking for another girl, the girl he chose was very risky, and her father was head of the police department. I told Shane this but he didn't listen, he grabbed her anyway, we bought her home a couple of days ago. She put up a fight and I had to drag her out the car. Shane lost his patience and killed her."

"I saw." He looked up at me, shocked by what I'd said.

"You saw?"

"Yes, I was watching by the window, I saw you drag her out, heard her cries and then the silence. But I didn't see what happened then."

"Well, Shane went to dig the grave, as always. I got drunk."

"Why does Shane dig the graves why doesn't he make you?"

"He thinks it helps his conscience, puts them to rest in the ground and out of his mind. He is twisted and sick. He likes control."

"How did the police know to be here?"

"I snuck out when he was sitting outside your door. Put in a call to the police and tipped them off to where they could find the missing girls."

"But why are they waiting outside the gates? Why didn't they break in?"

"I left them a note to not come past the gates, I knew Shane would have something in preparation to defend his life's work, there's no way he'd give it up so easily. I'm just glad they listened, otherwise there might have been more than one innocent soul lying dead on the grass."

"You mean that man with the gun was.., is Shane?" My face turned ashen,

"Do you think him incapable of cold-blooded murder?" he asked a strange tone on his voice. I couldn't make out his meaning. "It's ok, I understand. After all I was the one who came to you every night, not him, right?" the corner of his mouth turned up a little, disgusted. With himself or with me, it was hard to tell. "It doesn't matter now; the past is in the past." That comment angered me, it was fine for him to say that so matter-of-fact, but he didn't have to lie awake every night trembling with fear, or crouching in pain, or knocked unconscious. My fists tightened, I could feel the anger welling up inside, bubbling ferociously, what control I had over my anger was quickly slipping from my grasp.

"Why are you doing this?" I barked at him.

"Doing what?" he asked genuinely confused. That was a good question, what was he doing? I didn't even know. I didn't know who to trust, I'd thought myself almost in love with Shane, to find out now that he was lying, that he was the true monster. But was he? How could I trust Dimitri, after everything he has put me through? I needed to talk to Shane, to see what he would say. At that time though, I knew only one thing, I couldn't trust either of them, both monsters, both liars. Guilty until proven innocent. I had to get out of there, I had to be free. I could see only one way out in that moment, and it was Dimitri here with me in that minute. But I didn't have to trust him, keep your friends close, but your enemies closer, well, this was that moment right?

It was a few hours afterwards when things took a turn for the worse. Dimitri was curled up asleep in the corner of the room, I was lying on the bed but I wasn't asleep. My mind was running through all I could remember of my time here, I was trying so hard to find any clue, any hint that Shane was the monster, not Dimitri. I couldn't remember anything. If he was, then he was good; very good and didn't leave a trace of doubt in my memory. I went through all those dreadful nights and painful days. I was falling into an unsteady sleep when there were three loud bangs against the door; I opened my eyes quickly but very confused, were those happening in the present or was that a memory of one of those nights? I couldn't tell but Dimitri had sat bolt up-right in his chair, so it was real. Another bang, I mimicked Dimitri and shot upright onto the bed. The hinges of the door started to rattle under the strain of the heavy boots thudding against it.

Another thud and the screws came loose. Another thud, one hinge flew off the door and rattled onto the floor boards. The final thud sent the door flinging off its hinges and there in the doorway stood Shane. My heart stopped for a moment, when he stepped into the room, his image was that of a nightmare. Eyes wide and manic like the beast on a hunt. His face was smeared with blood; my eyes slowly took in everything. I'll never forget it. Clear as day. He was crazed. He bared his teeth, blood dripping from the side of his mouth. His white shirt had turned a mix of deep red and brown. His arms displayed under his rolled-up shirt sleeves a number of scars. I noticed then, to my horror, they were patterns carved into his skin, mostly by his own hand, roughly with jagged shapes, all freshly cut. Moving slowly down to his hands was the biggest shock of all. I heard Dimitri's sharp intake of breath next to me. In his left hand, he held the head of the girl who was shot down on the grass. Grasping it by the hair, he held it like a prize. Dimitri jumped off the bed and emptied his stomach onto the floor, I had to struggle not to join him and do the same. There was then complete silence, the three of us, standing perfectly still, no-one moved, no-one spoke. It was the calm before the storm.
I could no longer deny that Shane was the monster.

    It took me by complete surprise and I was knocked backwards off the bed as Shane threw the severed head right at me. He moved so quickly and so suddenly that I had not a chance of avoiding it. I sat on the floor in horror as it lay on my chest, staring into the dead, terrified eyes of a girl who only hours before I had rescued from the cellar. It was the girl who mistrusted me, Simone and maybe in hindsight she was right not to.

    Dimitri grabbed the blanket off the bed and threw it over the head, then he picked it up and placed it on the floor beside me before taking my hands and pulling me to my feet. He had to steady me; my legs were shaking so badly I fell to the floor a few times. Shane hadn't moved from the doorway. We were trapped and the only way out of that room was blocked by the last thing we wanted to get any closer to. Not a word said, Shane took two steps backwards and walked down the corridor. We left it a few moments before moving, but slowly we edged towards the door, Dimitri barely breathing, seemed in a state of calm-shock. I on the other hand was on the verge of a full-blown panic attack, my breathing was so heavy and fast I could hear nothing else. We hesitated going past the doorframe for fear of what he might have hidden out there. What traps he might have in plan for us. I looked Dimitri in the eye, and could see the same startled fear I had, he clenched his teeth and I nodded. We were in this together. He was now shaking, I could feel it through his arm which he had around my waist. We both took a deep breath, there was nothing for it, and we had but one choice. Out on the landing was complete silence; Shane was nowhere to be seen. We made quickly for the stairs, the opposite direction from where we saw Shane go. We took another glimpse behind us after a few steps and to our horror, out of no-where Shane had returned, we thought we had a chance, we were wrong, we didn't hear a sound as he appeared behind us. We just about made it to the top of the stairs, I don't know what it was but I felt something hard hit the back of my head. I felt sick to my stomach and everything began to slowly go dark. I'd fallen out of Dimitri's grasp and tumbled down the stairs, landing on my back. Just before I passed out I remember seeing Shane grab Dimitri by the hair and I heard shouts and cries as Dimitri tried to get loose, the thuds and thumps as he was dragged up the stairs to the next floor. Then all went black.

When I finally came around my sense were all blurry, my sight worse than all took the longest to return to me. The noises were clear as day, there were ear piercing screams coming from above and shouts and bangs coming from below. I tried to get up but I couldn't stand, so I pulled myself up the stairs. The screams were deafening and went straight through me. I'd managed to pull myself up the stairs and half-way along the corridor when everything went silent. The cries, the bangs and shouting; everything stopped. I hurried onwards, confused and dazed, starting on the second stair case that led to the third floor. There were drops of

blood leading the way so I followed those. The cries from above hadn't started again and panic kicked in, I hope I wasn't too late. I didn't know what I was going to do but I tried to stand again, the pain shot through my leg, my ankle had been broken in the fall and I couldn't put my weight on it but my body felt so numb anyway that I fell straight back down. I was getting so tired, but I made it up the next flight to the attic.
I'd never been up there before and for that I was hugely thankful. The door was open and hanging half off its hinges, I'd walked right into a nightmare. Another one. There was one table, and on it were a number of frightful, old tools, by the looks of it used for torture or punishment in the olden days, spread across in a hurried fashion, I tried to breath. Some to my horror were coated in fresh blood. I looked around the rest of the room, old and dusty, it wasn't used often. And then my blood ran cold, in the corner was a body, hanging limply from the wall, his arms chained and shackled to the wall above his head, he sat, his head slumped down almost to his chest. I took a small hesitant step towards him, then I noticed the carvings in the skin, this was Shane. So where was Dimitri? Then I heard chains rattle gently from the other corner, I took steps closer to the noise and found Dimitri in a similar state, one arm imprisoned in chains and shackled to the wall. Both men began to stir. I stood frozen and rooted to the spot. I didn't know what to do. So I did nothing.

Dimitri stirred and coughed, he splattered blood on the floor in front of him in an effort to breathe. I took a glance toward Shane, he hadn't moved so I edged towards Dimitri slowly, I lifted his head in an attempt to help him, he struggled to open his eyes, when he did he looked afraid. He seemed to recognise me, but his eyes were crazed and wide opened, darting all over the place and not focusing on me, eventually he settled to something just behind my right ear. I tried to turn but the fear I saw in his eyes began to well up inside me, oozing through my body like a parasite, paralyzing me. Dimitri tried to speak, but no words came out, just stutters, I turned my head and saw what he saw, standing above me, wielding a butcher's knife looming over me like a dark shadow in an alleyway at sunset was Shane, blood dripped down his arm and fell in a small puddle below. For what felt like an eternity, no-one moved. Three statues frozen in time, in a horror movie photo shoot. Then, all of a sudden Shane reached down and grabbed me by the throat, hoisting me up into the air until the tips of my toes barely touched the floor. Still gripping my neck he pulled me towards the middle of the room, where there hung two chains from the ceiling, he attached one chain to my left wrist, the other he put into a shackle attached to the other chain. The shackle had small needled ends along the inside, I felt them dig into my wrist as he tightened the shackle, the warm blood dripped down my arm, my throat seized with fear and the hands around them made no noise but I could hear Dimitri moaning, trying to tell me something. I watched as Shane released me and walked slowly towards the table of instruments, stoking them as he passed; he hovered over one, seemed to change his mind, moved onto another and repeated the process.

"Tell me Casey, why I should make your passing quick?" He stopped at my silence and looked towards me, when I still didn't answer he smirked and continued his search of the perfect weapon.

"Let me try another one then." He ran over to Dimitri "TELL ME THEN, WHY I SHOULD MAKE IT EASY FOR HIM." he untied Dimitri and threw him to the ground in front of me, kicking him a few times, Dimitri stayed down.

Again I said nothing. He picked up a pair of shears: "Speak or he will lose his fingers, one at a time." I tried to speak, the image of the poor girl's four fingers lying on the cell below rushed into my mind. The screams deafened me as one of Dimitri's fingers fell to the floor.

"Please" I sobbed, "Why are you doing this Shane?"

"Why? Why?" his anger increased, but he moved away from us, he flipped the table and the crash of tools fell to the floor.

"Why, did I get given away and trained to kill. Why was I taken from the loving home of my mother and thrown into this shit-hole while my sister was allowed to stay with her? Why, why, why. There are so many questions that begin that way. None of them will ever gain an answer." He moved towards me and laid a few blows to my stomach, I gripped the chain, the pins dug deeper into my arm.

"My filthy, murdering father, well, he didn't last long, I killed him eventually, slowly. I had him begging me for mercy, the tears and screams were music to my ears!" he began to conduct an orchestra only he could hear. He seemed to forget anyone else was in the room, and then he stopped. He turned, his eyes alight with a new malice, he was crazy, he picked up the nearest weapon, a whip and kicking Dimitri roughly aside came straight for me, the leather rope made contact with my stomach, the burning, blistering pain seared through my body and loosened my vocal chords, I let out a scream. Dimitri stirred with the noise. Shane smiled and hit again, and again, and again until I had no energy left to scream.

"Why me?" I managed weakly with my failing breath

"Why you, Casey? I ask that every day. Why did they keep you and not me? What makes you so special?" He was barely making sense,

"What?"

"I am you brother Casey, my father is your father. But of course you have the joy of never having met him."

"My brother?" I said my face as white as a ghost.

"Yes, I am your brother. I took you from your home all those years ago, I murdered mother and father and I locked you in this house."

"But Dimitri, he.. he was the one who.."

"Yes, he does seem the type doesn't him? Easily persuaded, and weak, he did whatever I told him to do, coward." He kicked him again. "And now, he will lay there and once again watch as I 'make music' help less to do anything." Where he got the knife from I didn't see but I felt it as it touched my temple, he slanted it and pulled it slowly down the side of my face, the pain was unbearable, everything in the room flashed and started to fade slowly, as it spun around me, I heard a crash, shouting and three gun shots, I saw Shane stumble backward. I felt a hand touch my neck, and then everything went dark.

JUNE 20TH 2017

My eyes were heavy and hard to open. My head was groggy and pain began to flood into every nerve in my body as it slowly awoke. The sunlight shone on my face, I blinked ferociously as it blinded me. I tried to move but I couldn't. My mind raced and flew, I tried to understand where I was, but I was so confused, images were flashing, overlapping and flying around my mind as I tried to piece them together into one picture or timeline, an overwhelming fear took over and before I could stop it I screamed. Hands came rushing to me, holding my arms and legs, the pain was severe,

"Casey, you are safe. You are in hospital. Casey, Casey, breath."

The voice was calm and gentle, but who it belonged to I couldn't see, my fear didn't die down but the panic calmed, slowly I settled down trying to make sense of anything. My mind was in sensory overload. I tried to talk but it only choked me, then I realised I had a tube down my throat, a different panic set in and I started coughing. A doctor rushed in and removed the tubes; the fresh air rushed in and filled my lungs. By then my eyesight had returned to normal, the sunlight, now not so blinding, lit up the room. I could see the doctor and two nurses and a man, who looked familiar, and two police officers in uniform. It started to dawn on me that I was lying in a hospital bed. The man in the suit made his way towards me.

"Casey, my name is detective Danvers. I would like to say on behalf of my daughter, and on behalf of the parents of the other girls, thank you. Thank you for saving them."

"Where's-, what happened? Shane, Dimitri, we were, we were—"

"Ssshh, it's ok Casey, you are safe. They are both dead."
"What happened?"
"You don't need to know just now, rest."
"Please," his hand was touching the sheets of my bed; I reached out and held his hand. "Please, tell me, I need to know."

He hesitated, but nodded signaled to the others to leave the room and took a seat beside me.

"If you want me to stop, if it gets too much, just let me know." He gave a small encouraging and comforting smile. I tried to return it.

"Casey, when we found you, you had passed out. Shane had beaten you badly. We heard the screams from the drive way, and rushed to the house, the door, we tried to open but it had been jammed and blocked from the inside and getting through proved more difficult than we thought. Then the screams went silent. We feared the worse. We'd seen you running out behind the other girls and when that poor girl was shot dead, we saw the man grab you and drag you back into the house. We knew you were still in there somewhere, but we did fear the worse. Then when we heard your screams we knew we had to be quick. We used full force and made it through the back door; we rushed up to the attic and found you hanging by your wrists. Shane was standing beside you with a knife, covered in blood. We told Shane to drop the weapon but he made no attempt to comply, instead he turned back to you, so we shot a few times. He died there at the scene. Dimitri had dragged himself toward you but in the confusion we believed him to be an accomplice of Shane, we feared he was trying to finish what Shane didn't and shot him before he had the chance to. We rushed you to the hospital just in time. You've been asleep for four days. Your wounds will take time to heal. But you are safe now. Sleep Casey. We will talk more when you are feeling better. Everything will be revealed to you. You must have many questions." He nodded toward me, squeezed my hand and then walked out the room.

Everything he told me was whirling through my mind; the memories of that night were just out of my reach. It felt like I was trying to piece together black spots of my memory based on the tales of other people, what they told me felt real and true, but they were, at the moment, merely images my mind created to match what I've been told. I tried to push these thoughts aside and sighed a breath of relief, I was free. I was safe. I closed my eyes and the image of their bodies lying on the ground, two captors, two monsters, two friends and two enemies, a lover, and a brother. Two misunderstood and mistreated young boys, created to be killers. I tried to remember what Shane had told me in that room, could it really be true? Could he really be my brother? There were so many questions flooding around my mind, new emotions sparking rage and anger through me. Emotions I didn't know how to deal with. Questions I knew in time would be answered, but for now I was safe and that was all that mattered. For the first time in my life I felt safe. Whoever they were, their past was irrelevant, they were dead and I was safe, surrounded by doctors and police. I closed my eyes and for the first time in all my memory, I slept soundly.

JULY 3RD 2017

It's been two weeks since I woke up in that hospital bed. My wounds are healing well, slowly, but well and I now spend my time in a personal room, all my own on one of the wards here at the hospital, I am putting pen to paper and writing down my memories of the events of the last few weeks, my diary, it seems remains in the house, under my mattress much emptier than this new one. It's amazing how so much can change in the course of just a few weeks. I was captive and now I am free, although I remain a captive of my own memories and emotions. Reliving the horrors of this month, not to mention the tangle of webs of the earlier years I have still to wade through. Many, remain dormant in my mind, blocked out and hidden and until I find the strength and courage to open those doors, they wait, impatiently to be released from the bottle I've suppressed them into.

I feel like I am standing on the edge of a cliff; before me, a vast open ocean; behind me, a fierce tidal wave. The first represents the future, a glimmer of hope for a new start, many miles away on the horizon, all I have to do is jump and let the current take me the rest of the way. The later, represents the haunting, harrowing memories of a past I am so desperate to be free of and yet which remains shackled to me, locked to it with no key. No matter how far I run, it is always there. There is one choice before me, step forward, or step back. Step forward with a chance, all I have to do is take the leap, trust I will avoid all rocks on the way down, and believe I can navigate the merciless waves as they crash upon the cliff side. But take a step backwards, and I'll be swept away by the past, engulfed by its power and resilience, a hopeless, impossible battle of keeping head above water. Or do I take the third option? Take neither a step back nor a step forward. A lifetime stuck in one spot, surviving, but never living. Frozen in time, blinded to what lies ahead and yet denying what is coming up behind.

How do I begin to piece together the shattered shards of a broken life? When the foundations of everything around me come crumbling down and I am left utterly exposed to the harsh realities of life, where then do I start? To be thrust so suddenly onto a new path, out of the shadows and heading to light, how do I keep my footing and not fall, to not be dragged down by the chains and shackles that I will not, or cannot yet release. Does the past define who I am? Does it define who I will become? Am I only defined by what I have survived, a victim, a survivor, can I not just be alive?

There is only one clear choice that must be taken, the leap of faith. A storm is coming whether I want it or not, I may as well meet it like an old friend.

To be continued….

Printed in Great Britain
by Amazon